MABELA THE CLEVER

RETOLD BY MARGARET READ MACDONALD

ILLUSTRATED BY TIM COFFEY

ALBERT WHITMAN & COMPANY

MORTON GROVE, ILLINOIS

A cautionary tale for Julie, Tom, Jenny, Nat, and all their little mouselings, from Mama, who learned her wisdom from Grandpa Murray and Grandma Millie.—M. R. M.

For my dad.—T. C.

Library of Congress Cataloging-in-Publication Data
MacDonald, Margaret Read, 1940-
Mabela the clever / Retold by Margaret Read MacDonald; illustrated by Tim Coffey.
p. cm.
Summary: An African folktale about a mouse who pays close attention
to her surroundings and avoids being tricked by the cat.
ISBN 0-8075-4902-9 (hardcover)
[1. Folklore — Africa.] I. Coffey, Tim, ill. II. Title. PZ8.1.M15924 Mab 2000
398.2'096'04529353—dc21 00-008307

Published in 2001 by Albert Whitman & Company, 6340 Oakton Street, Morton Grove, Illinois 60053-2723.
Published simultaneously in Canada by General Publishing, Limited, Toronto.

Printed in China.
10 9 8 7 6 5 4

The display typeface is FC-Nueland Inline regular.
The text typeface is Woodland ITC medium.
The illustrations were rendered in acrylic on watercolor paper textured with gesso.
The design is by Scott Piehl.

THIS STORY has been elaborated through many tellings. It began when I first read a story in Ruth Finnegan's LIMBA STORIES AND STORYTELLING (Oxford, England: Oxford University Press, 1967) called "The Clever Cat." The story was collected in 1964 from Kirinkoma Konteh, a young man of Kamabai, Sierra Leone, Africa.

Dr. Finnegan tells us that stories are very important to the Limba people. They tell hundreds of tales and use them to pass on traditional wisdom and morals. Long before there were written books, knowledge was passed from parent to child through these tales. The Limba say "Our heart's memory is our book." Maybe you can place this story of Mabela the Clever in your heart's memory to share with someone else someday.

You might enjoy playing a Mabela game. The players who are "mice" march along in a straight line, singing, with "Mabela" in the front. No one looks back. The "Cat" follows behind. Every time the mice sing "Fo Feng," the cat catches the mouse at the end of the line. All the "caught" mice line up behind the cat. Everyone keeps singing until all the mice but Mabela are caught.

I don't know how the Limba song would have sounded, so I've made up my own tune. (Or you can make up a tune yourself.)

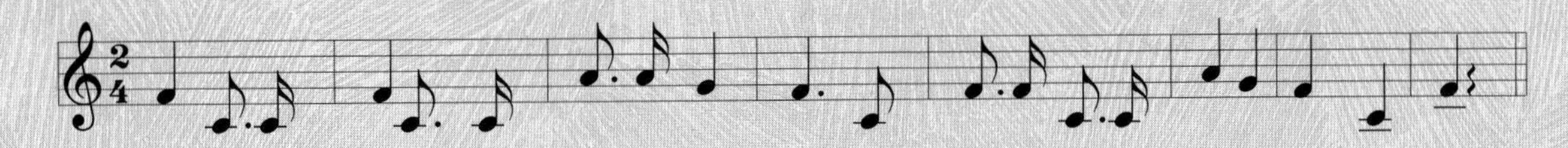

IN THE EARLY TIMES, some were clever and some were foolish. The Cat was one of the clever ones. The mice were mostly foolish.

But one little mouse was not so foolish. Her name was Mabela, and her father had taught her cleverness.

Her father always told her, "Mabela, when you are out and about, keep your ears open and LISTEN.

"Mabela, when you are out and about, keep your eyes open and LOOK AROUND YOU.

"Mabela, when you are speaking, PAY ATTENTION TO WHAT YOU ARE SAYING.

"Mabela, if you have to move, MOVE FAST!"

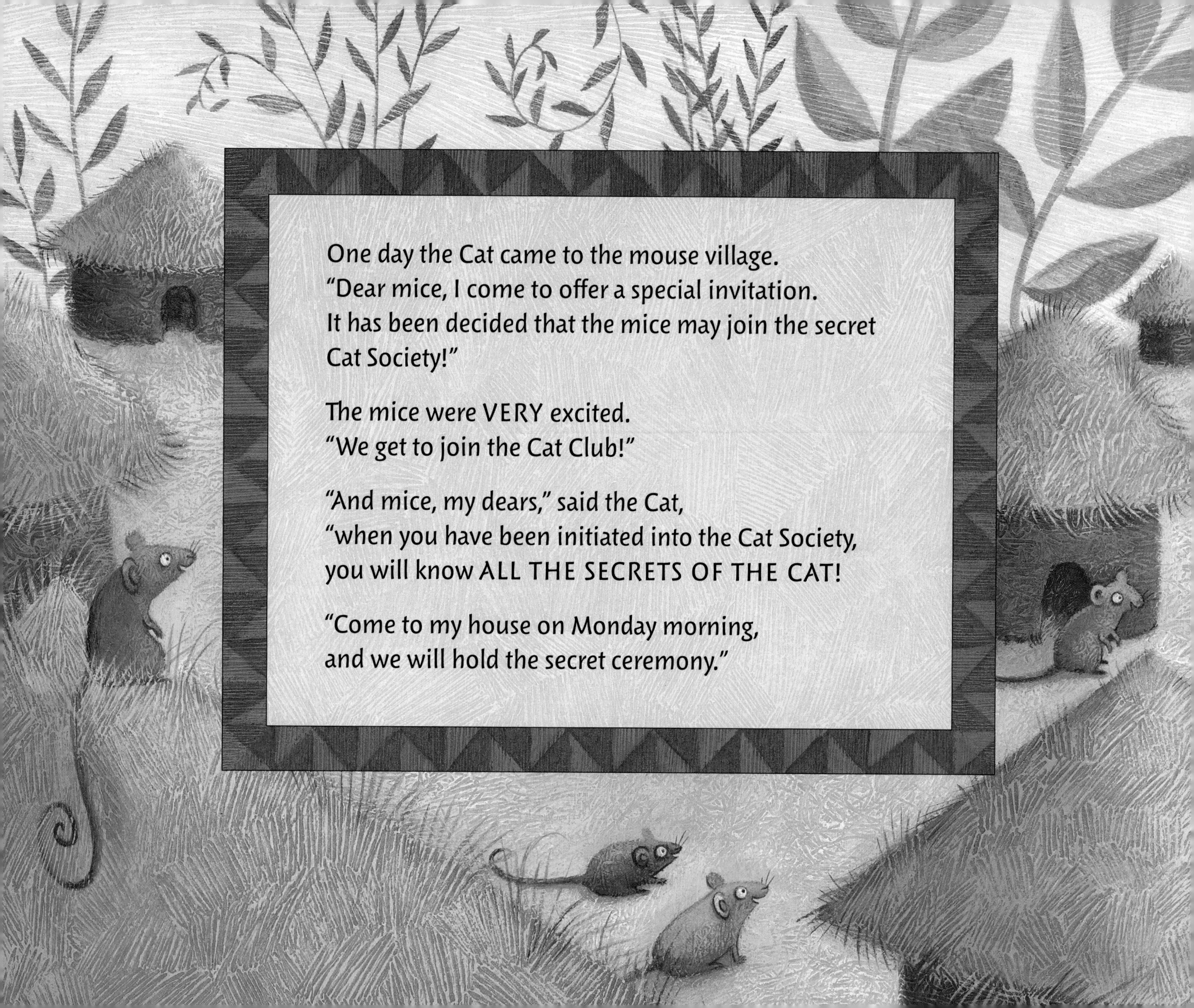

One day the Cat came to the mouse village.
"Dear mice, I come to offer a special invitation.
It has been decided that the mice may join the secret
Cat Society!"

The mice were VERY excited.
"We get to join the Cat Club!"

"And mice, my dears," said the Cat,
"when you have been initiated into the Cat Society,
you will know ALL THE SECRETS OF THE CAT!

"Come to my house on Monday morning,
and we will hold the secret ceremony."

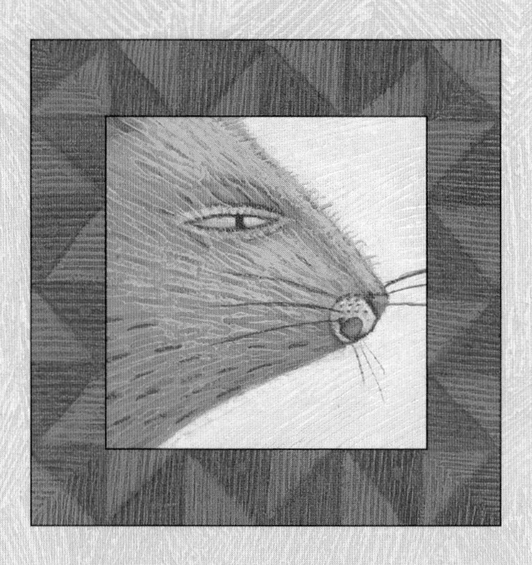

Monday morning bright and early, the little mice were there.

"Oh, my, you have ALL arrived!" said the Cat. "How delicious…
I mean, how delightful. You must all learn the secret Cat Society song. The song goes like this…

WHEN WE ARE MARCHING,
WE NEVER LOOK BACK!
THE CAT IS AT THE END,
FO FENG!
FO FENG!

The little mice learned to shout loudly on the last **FO FENG!**

The Cat lined them up in a straight line.
And at the end came … the CAT.
Mabela got to march in the front because she was the smallest of all.

“Now we will march into the forest,” called the Cat, “and you will learn the secrets of the Cat. Remember, you must never, ever look back!”

Off they started.
Mabela was leading the way
so proudly.

**WHEN WE ARE MARCHING,
WE NEVER LOOK BACK!
THE CAT IS AT THE END,
FO FENG!
FO FENG!**

When we are marching,
we NEVER look back!
The Cat is at the end,
fo feng!
FO FENG!

Every time the mice shouted **FO FENG!** the cat FO FENGED another mouse!

Suddenly Mabela remembered.
Her father had always said, "Mabela, when you are out and about,
keep your ears open and LISTEN."

Mabela stopped singing for a moment and listened.
She did not hear a long line of mice behind her. She heard a FEW mice.
And the Cat's voice was getting closer each time they sang **FO FENG!**

Then Mabela remembered something else her father always said. "Mabela, when you are out and about, keep your eyes open and LOOK AROUND YOU."

Mabela turned her head just a little to the left, just a little to the right. She did NOT see a LONG line of mice. She saw a SHORT line of mice and the CAT VERY CLOSE!

Then she remembered that her father had said,
"Mabela, when you are speaking,
PAY ATTENTION TO WHAT YOU ARE SAYING."
She listened to her song.

WHEN WE ARE MARCHING,
WE NEVER LOOK BACK!
THE CAT IS AT THE END . . .

Mabela stopped. The Cat is at the end?
What does that mean? It means . . .
NO ONE IS WATCHING THE CAT!
Mabela turned right around. There was the Cat!
She had just FO FENGED the mouse behind Mabela!

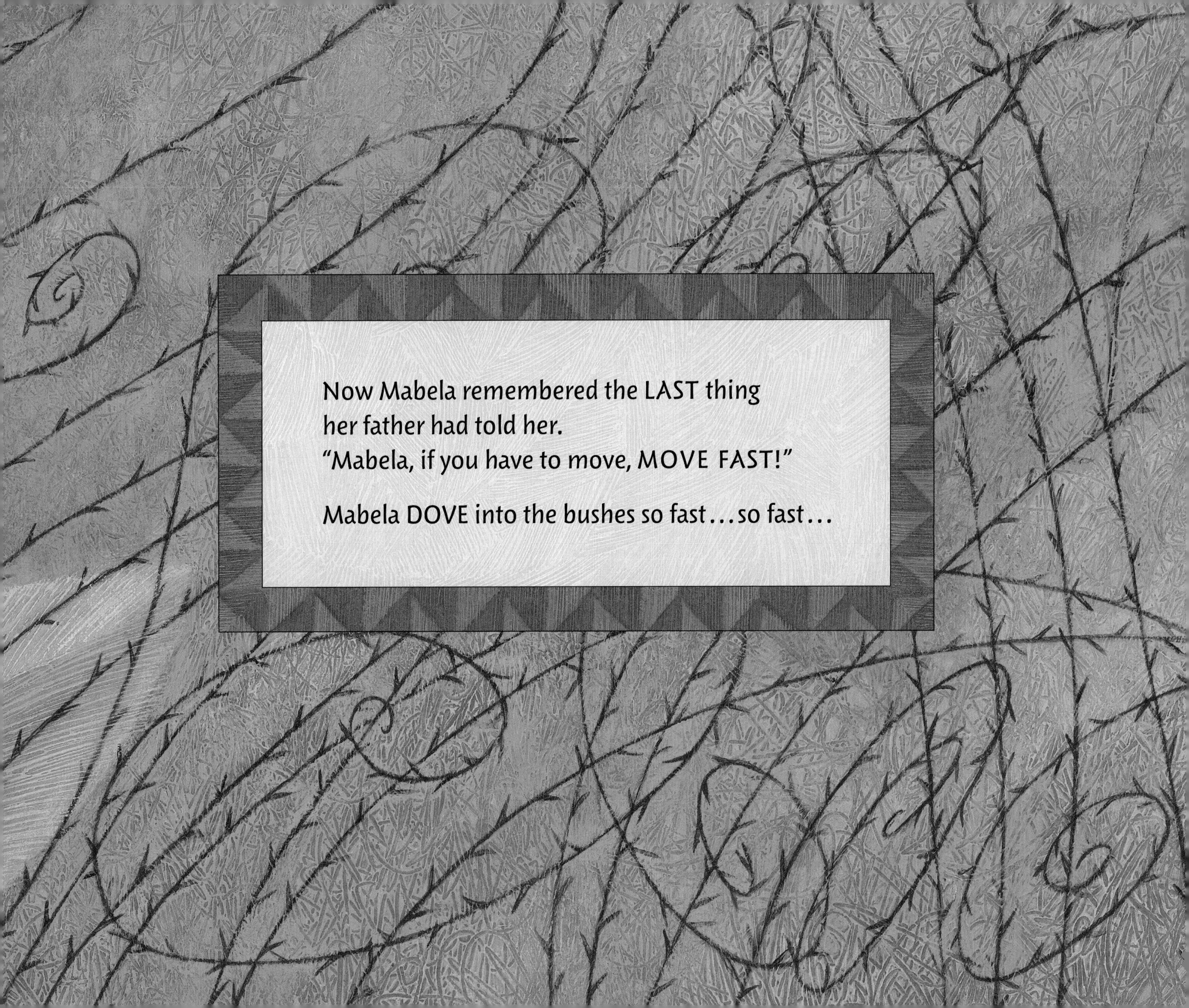

Now Mabela remembered the LAST thing
her father had told her.
"Mabela, if you have to move, MOVE FAST!"

Mabela DOVE into the bushes so fast…so fast…

the Cat pounced on nothing but thorns!

The Cat was stuck,
the mice were out,
and Mabela lived to
tell the tale.

She told it to her children.
And her children's children.

Limba parents are STILL telling this story to their children.
It is good to remember the things Mabela's father taught her.
"When you are out and about, keep your ears open and LISTEN.
When you are out and about, keep your eyes open and LOOK AROUND YOU.
When you are speaking, PAY ATTENTION TO WHAT YOU ARE SAYING.
And...if you have to move, MOVE FAST!"

Limba grandparents say, "If a person is clever,
it is because someone has taught them their cleverness."